Written by Emily Gale

Illustrated by Mark Marshall

First published by Parragon in 2008
Parragon
Queen Street House
4 Queen Street
Bath BA1 1HE, UK

Copyright © Parragon Books Ltd 2008

All rights reserved. No part of this publication may be reproduced, stored in a retrieval system or transmitted, in any form or by any means, electronic, mechanical, photocopying, recording or otherwise, without the prior permission of the copyright holder.

ISBN 978-1-4075-1841-1

Printed in China

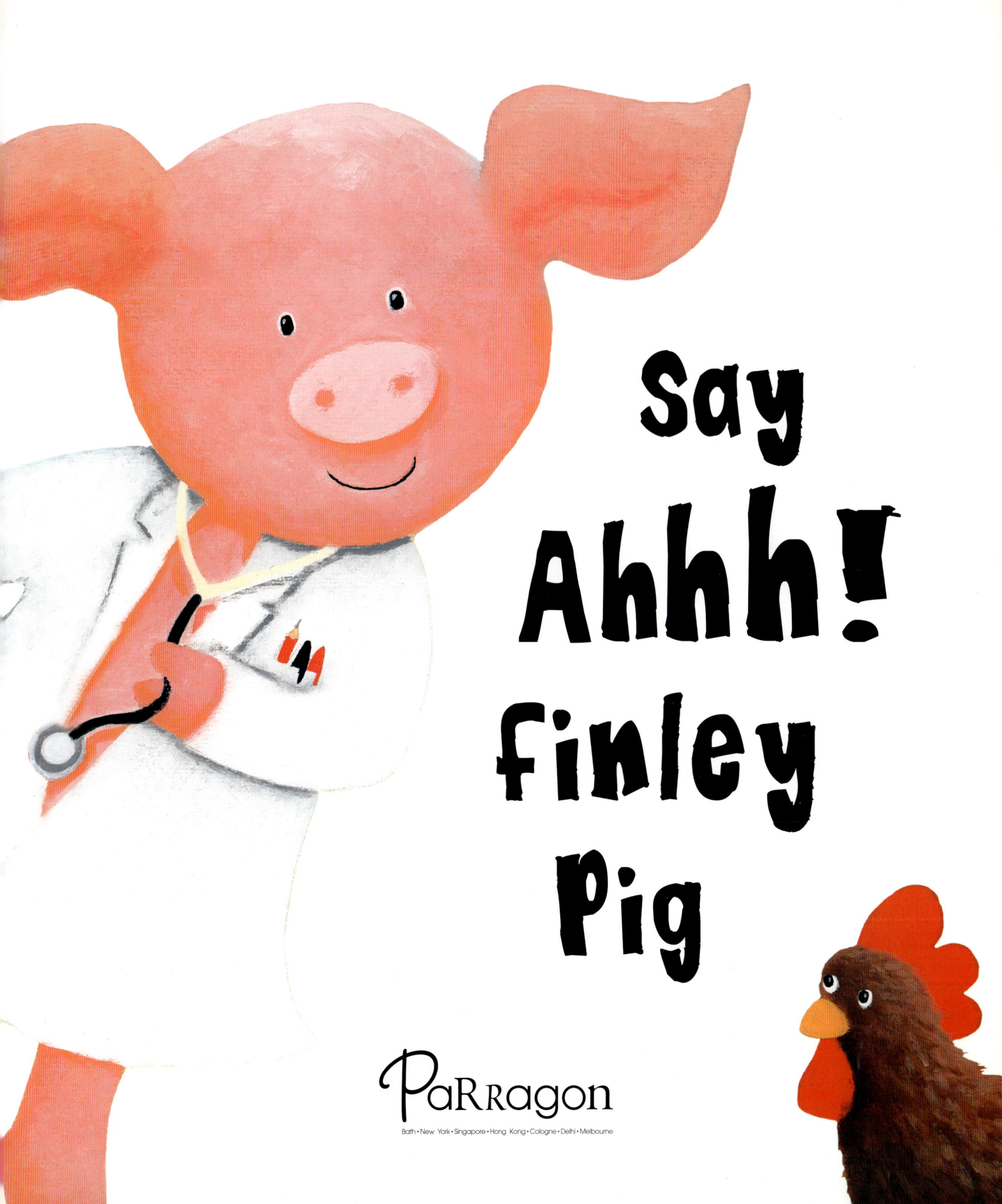

Say Ahhh! Finley Pig

PaRragon
Bath · New York · Singapore · Hong Kong · Cologne · Delhi · Melbourne

Finley Pig was happy.

"It's alright for some!" said Agatha Chicken who was always sticking her beak in. "This is a busy farm, Lazybones," she clucked.

"I'm not Lazybones, I'm Finley."

"Cheeky pig!" Agatha flapped her wings, and squawked until Finley ran away.

Finley sat under a tree to think.
Mud baths were lovely, but he did want
to be a big help on the busy farm.
What would he be good at?

"I've got it!"

Mommy Pig was puzzled.
"Where are you going with all that, Finley?"

"It's not Finley, it's Doctor Pig! And I'm late for my first patient."

"Don't say moo, say ahhh!" said Finley.

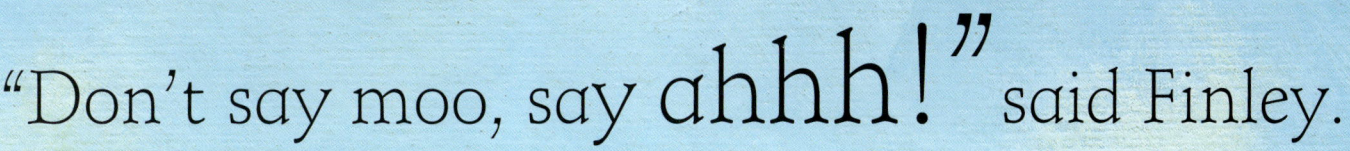

"Finley, there's nothing wrong with my leg."

Chester Sheep was not good at having his heart listened to—he wouldn't stop munching.

The geese, Heidi and Dora, refused their medicine.

The sheepdog... ran away.

Being a doctor was really hard work, but the most difficult patients of all were...

... the chickens.

At the end of a long day, Mommy Pig was pleased to see Finley.

"I'm very good at being a doctor," said Finley. "But I'm . . .

"... even better at being me.

Do Not Disturb